Christmas in the Barn

by Margaret Wise Brown · illustrated by Diane Goode

HarperCollinsPublishers

Christmas in the Barn • Text copyright ©1952 by Margaret Wise Brown • Text copyright renewed 1980 by Albert Clark
Illustrations copyright © 2004 by Diane Goode • Manufactured in China by South China Printing Company Ltd. • All rights reserved. • www.harperchildrens.com
Library of Congress Cataloging-in-Publication Data Brown, Margaret Wise, 1910–1952. Christmas in the barn / by Margaret Wise Brown ; illustrated by Diane Goode.— 1st ed. p.   cm. Summary: Lyrical text
relates the birth of a child in a barn among the animals, with illustrations which depict the barn and people of a present-day farm. ISBN 0-06-052634-3 — ISBN 0-06-052635-1 (lib. bdg.) [1. Christmas—
Fiction. 2. Stories in rhyme.] I. Goode, Diane, ill. II. Title. PZ8.3.B815Co 2004 2003017481 [E]—dc22 CIP AC • Typography by Stephanie Bart-Horvath • 1 2 3 4 5 6 7 8 9 10 • ❖ • First Edition

In a big warm barn in an ancient field

The oxen lowed, the donkey squealed,

The horses stomped, the cattle sighed,

And quietly the daylight died in the sunset of the west.

And a star rose brighter than all stars in the sky.

The field mice scampered in the hay

And two people who had lost their way
Walked into the barn at the end of the day

And they were allowed to sleep in the hay

"Because there was no room in the inn."

The little mice rustled in the sweet dry grass
Near the lambs and the kine and the ox and the ass.

The horses pawed the golden straw,
The little donkey brayed "Hee Haw,"

And there they were all safe and warm

All together in that ancient barn

When hail—the first wail of a newborn babe reached the night

Where one great star was burning bright

And shepherds with their sheep

Are come to watch him sleep.

What child is this who is born here

Where the oxen stomp and peer,

Away in a manger, no crib for his bed

What child is this who lays down his sweet head?

In the big warm barn in the ancient field

The little child sleeps, the donkey squeals

The star goes down

Yet the wise men stay to see the dawning Christmas Day.

The child was sleeping in the hay
And there they were
All safe and warm

All together
In that ancient barn.